Cat and Rat Fall Out

Written by Geraldine McCaughrean

Illustrated by Klaas Verplancke

This is a story from Africa. It tells us why cats and rats are not the best of friends.

A long, long time ago, Cat and Rat were great friends. They had to be friends because they lived all alone on a little island. They stayed on the island because the sea lay all around, and Cat and Rat did not like to get wet.

In the middle of the island stood a big
tree. Each day, Cat climbed up and ate the
fruit on the tree. Each day, Rat dug down
and gnawed the root of the tree.

All day, every day, Rat gnawed root and Cat ate fruit.

"Cats like fruit," said Cat.

"Rats like root," said Rat.

Years went by, and every day
Cat ate fruit and Rat gnawed root.

One day Cat said, "I'm bored."

"I'm bored, too," said Rat.

"Fruit is boring," said Cat.

"You think fruit is boring?" said Rat.
"Root is boring, BORING! Gnawing is boring."

"Climbing is boring, too," agreed Cat.
"This island is boring."

Then Rat had an idea. "Let's leave this islar
and travel the world. The world may be full o
better things to eat."

"How can we go?" asked Cat. "We both
hate water."

"We will make a boat," said Rat.

"How clever you are," said Cat.
"I am glad I have you for a friend."

So Cat and Rat made a boat.
They made it out of a big tree root.

"Make it hollow, Rat, so that we can sit
in it," said clever Cat. So Rat gnawed away
at the root until it was hollow.

"Make a sail, Cat," said clever Rat.

So Cat made a sail and
wore it on her tail.

Then they jumped in and sailed away.
Soon their little island lay far, far away.
After a while, Cat said, "I'm hungry."
"Maybe we are not so clever," said Rat.
"We forgot to bring any food."

Now Cat was hungry and she longed
for some fruit. Now Rat was hungry
and he longed for some root.

"Go to sleep," said Rat. "Nobody is hungry
when they are asleep."

So Cat went to sleep. Rat did not. Well, the boat was made of root, wasn't it?

Rat gnawed the oar. Rat bit into the boat. Rat nibbled.

Cat woke up. "Don't eat the boat, you silly Rat! We will sink!"

"Sorry," said Rat. "Go back to sleep. I won't gnaw anymore."

So Cat went back to sleep.

Rat did not.

Rat gnawed some more of the oar.

He bit deeper into the boat.

Rat made a hole – *whoops!*

Sea water came in through the hole.
Cat woke up wet. Then Cat got angry and
scratched Rat. Rat bit Cat.

Cat batted Rat until he was almost flat.
The boat just bubbled. Then it sank.

Cat swam and Rat swam.

Luckily, they both got to land alive.

There they lay, on the sand, in the sun, side by side.

"Wait till I get dry," hissed Cat.

Rat did not wait.
He had seen Cat's claws
and Cat's sharp teeth.
Rat ran.

Rat is still running, even today.
And Cat is never far behind.